Solomon Levi MacKeefer

A Gypsy with a Very Great Heart

Author of *A Pound of Butter*
GORDON PLANEDIN

Solomon Levi MacKeefer

A Gypsy with a Very Great Heart

Author of *A Pound of Butter*
GORDON PLANEDIN

ARPress
45 Dan Road Suite 15
Canton MA 02021
 Hotline: 1(888) 821-0229
 Fax: 1(508) 545-7580

Ordering Information:
Quantity sales. Special discounts are available on quantity purchases by corporations, associations, and others. For details, contact the publisher at the address above.

Printed in the United States of America.

ISBN-13:   Softcover   979-8-89676-393-2
             eBook   979-8-89676-394-9
             Hardback 979-8-89676-395-6

Library of Congress Control Number: 2025920942

To my sweetheart, Mary, with thanks given
for the help of my daughter, Karen Planedin;
my grandsons, Gordon Shaw and Ryan Cook;
and our friend Cate Albrecht.

I had spent a long and tiring morning trying to catch a ride when finally a car pulled over and waited for me to walk up and crawl inside. The driver had a big friendly smile on his face as he greeted me and informed me that he was traveling another forty miles to the next town. I leaned back and relaxed in the comfortable, air-conditioned interior for a much-needed rest.

During the ride he commented that he could drop me off at a place called Solly's Bar and Grill if I was broke and hungry—the owner was a kindhearted fellow who might be able to help me out. When we hit the next town, he dropped me off at Solly's, which was a fairly nice-looking place. Before the driver left, he told me to go in and look for the owner, a guy named Bud.

I had no trouble finding Bud since he was the only one there. He told me that first he would make me some breakfast and then get me organized to cut some lawns outside. After a nice meal of bacon, eggs, and pancakes, we went outside. I was given a nice riding mower to use, and I was on the job. When I had finished the lawns, he poured me a beer and presented me with a proposition. He had lost the help of a senior because of health problems, and he needed someone to clean the building in the mornings. Since he had a small guest cottage in the yard, I could stay in it. It seemed like a very good deal.

At first he would come in the early morning and help me get organized. When I was able to do it myself, he gave me a set of keys, and I was on my own. I would let myself in, do a bit of work, make myself coffee and breakfast, and then get back to work. By opening time, I would have the restaurant ready to go.

During the day I was free to go and tour the town or just sleep most of the day. It seemed like a strange situation since I was under the impression that all licensed establishments stayed open until midnight.

This place was usually emptying out by ten thirty or eleven, and then Bud would close up.

The beauty of the situation was that we could sit and sip on a beer or two and he could tell me about the town. Since he had lived there all his life, he seemed to know it all. This is how I learned the story of Solly MacKeefer.

He was a gypsy, part of a gypsy band. His name was Solomon Levi Brown. His coming was not a part of his parents' plans but was more of an example of the old saying that "accidents cause people." As a consequence, he ended up as a child of the whole band of gypsies, dined with anyone handy, and slept wherever he could lay his head.

He spent his growing-up years traveling with the band and being involved with their activities. When they found a new location, the band would start setting up their tents to provide fortune-telling and other activities to generate some revenue. At the same time, the young ones would scope out the area to see whether there was any potential to steal a few chickens or other small animals in the middle of the night for food.

Among the band it was not considered a crime; rather, it was looked upon as playing a game. Since the gypsies were known as beggars and thieves, it was a question of who could prove to be the smarter. Since it was part of their lifestyle, it was inevitable that the gypsy would come out on top.

Solly's undoing was when some boys from the band went into the village and tried to steal a large turkey. They choked the bird to death but were unable to carry the prize away, because a large dog came out and put the run on the gang. The owners did not become aware of the episode until the next morning, when their daughter, who had raised the bird as a pet, found it dead on the lawn.

Solly happened to be walking by at that unfortunate time and saw the young girl totally distraught over the loss of her pet. Seeing that total despair in the child triggered something in Solly. He realized this was not some kind of a game but a major loss that would be with that child for the rest of her life.

From that time on, it became impossible for him to take part in chicken stealing. That episode affected him for the rest of his life.

Shortly thereafter he became acquainted with a man known as Old Anton, who was in the profession of repairing footwear and was even capable of building new shoes. Anton was a very interesting fellow, so Solly started spending more and more time with him. He helped Anton and learned the shoe trade.

One day while the small caravan was camped in a farmer's field near Liverpool, Solly discovered that his parents had moved on without leaving a forwarding address. So he moved in with Anton.

With Anton's encouragement, Solly started attending a small school nearby. Traveling was becoming harder and harder because of population growth, so the gypsies had to be prepared for change. Education was an obvious help.

At school he became acquainted with an attractive and very interesting young lady named Maria, who was just a few months younger than Solly. Before too long they became inseparable. Shortly after his nineteenth birthday, they built an addition to Anton's trailer and moved in together. Their life with Anton was one of peace and tranquility until old Anton got an infection. He sadly went to meet his maker and left Solly with his trailer and his shoe repair supplies and equipment.

Another good friend Solly acquired was the son of the farmer whose land they were staying on. Jeremiah MacKeefer was a few years older than Solly, but they got along in excellent fashion and shared many good thoughts. Solly and Maria lived a quiet and peaceful life on the farm in exchange for produce and a little bit of money.

In their discussions Jeremiah would often mention the fact that he could see no future on the farm. He mentioned that he would like to emigrate to Canada and suggested that Solly should also consider that option.

Since Solly had never acquired a birth certificate, Jeremiah suggested a midwife in the area who sometimes provided information to authorities to enable someone to obtain a certificate. She charged a fee for her service, but it was well worth the sum. He also advised Solly that he would be better off if she would name a birthplace somewhere in England since it was much easier for a British subject to emigrate to Canada.

When Solly became aware that they would be blessed with their first child, the concern for the future became more urgent, and he proceeded with the process of acquiring a birth certificate.

For the sum of twenty-five pounds, the midwife started the process toward that objective. Shortly after their daughter arrived healthy and smiling, he was pleased to come into possession of a certificate of birth for himself. For simplicity's sake he registered as a British subject under the name Solomon Levi MacKeefer. Shortly after their daughter Sarah's third birthday, Jeremiah's father passed on, and Jeremiah proceeded with the sale of the farm.

Within seven months Jeremiah had disposed of the farm and had received his documentation to emigrate to Canada. He assured Solly and Maria that he would be willing to help them join him in the new world.

Since the farm had been sold, it became more urgent to relocate, and so Solly proceeded to apply for the necessary emigration documentation. His new birth certificate listed him as Jeremiah's brother, and this seemed to speed up the emigration process. It now showed that he wanted to rejoin his relatives in Canada.

In less than ten months, he received the notification that his application had been approved.

Shortly after, Jeremiah informed Solly that he had located a rental property that had living quarters on the outskirts of town. It also had a provision where he could operate a shoe repair shop, and it was close to a school for Sarah.

It seemed that the wait was forever, but then one day they were on the ship with their meager possessions, excited to be on their journey to their new life.

The next thing they knew, they were at the dock, going through customs, and then riding in Jeremiah's van on their way to their new home.

Then there came the excitement of moving in and having their first meal at home. Solly was slowly able to get his shoe repair business into operation, and it was reassuring to see revenue start to come in.

As the years went by, Sarah did great in school, and the business slowly improved.

At this point, Maria realized that she had too much time on her hands. Since they were facing onto a street, she suggested that she could set up a fortune-telling booth and possibly bring in more revenue. Since she had learned a lot from the elder women in the gypsy band, she just needed to not see customers with any major problems. They both decided to go ahead with this plan. She slowly acquired some customers, and she also had something to occupy her time.

One day started like every other, with Sarah off to school, Maria at her fortune-telling booth, and Solly heading across town to his supplier to acquire materials.

Around ten in the morning, two young lads came wandering into the store. It was obvious that these youth needed some money to acquire some drugs, and seeing Maria was a fortune-teller, they worked on the assumption that gypsies always have some gold.

On this basis, they must have thought it was their lucky day. While the first one proceeded to lock the door, the other one made sure the drapes were closed. The first one grabbed Maria by the arm, dragged her into the living quarters, and proceeded to inform her that if she didn't come up with the stash of gold, she would be in big trouble.

Knowing not to argue, Maria produced her handbag containing about sixty-five dollars, which was all she had. But this was not enough, especially when they were expecting gold.

Then the guy gave her a violent blow to the head, which caused her to fall over onto the bed, and when they saw her there with her skirt up and exposing her legs, their interest changed from gold to other things.

They both took turns at raping her while subjecting her to more violent abuse. After using her for a couple of hours, they proceeded out the back door to escape.

When Sarah came home from school, she found the back door half-open. When she made her way in, she found her mother lying on the floor in a pool of her own blood, all bruised and in extreme pain.

Sarah was immediately on the phone calling for help, and then she was down on her knees beside her mother trying to comfort her. The police arrived in minutes, and Solly was there very soon after. The ambulance did not arrive for another ten minutes, and when it showed up, the medics quickly loaded Maria inside and sped off to the hospital.

Solly and Sarah followed behind in the police car. When they finally reached the hospital, they were unable to be with Maria in the room, as the staff were busy administering to her condition. In the process, Maria kept drifting in and out of consciousness. During the examination the doctors found some cracked ribs, along with other bruising, and they had concerns that the broken ribs could have caused damage to her lungs, as she seemed to be having trouble breathing.

Once Maria was finally stabilized, Sarah and Solly were able to join her so they could comfort her as much as possible. Even then, it was obvious that she was in extreme pain and suffering greatly and that her situation was very grave.

The worst part of it was that there was no option to operate; they could only hope that her immune system would pull her through. Solly and Sarah stayed with her through the night, holding on to her and trying to provide as much support as they could; however, it seemed like her attackers had broken her spirit and destroyed her will to live. As the sun was breaking through the clouds, she must have grabbed on to one of its rays and gone on to a place where there was no hatred or violence, only peace.

For Sarah and Solly there was nothing left other than to hold on to each other for comfort. They were heartbroken, but they knew that if Maria could have survived but all crippled up for life, she would have sooner preferred to be a free spirit instead.

They sat there in silence for a while, and then Solly went to find a phone so he could call Jeremiah to come and get them. The front desk informed Solly that as soon as they received clearance from the authorities, they would contact Solly as to the future process regarding Maria. In the meantime, after considering the options, Solly decided that they preferred cremation so Maria's remains could stay with them.

It took some time before the team of investigators were finished with their examination of Solly's residence and Solly and Sarah were able to go to get their possessions. Solly now was certain that he needed to get Sarah away from the city, and he wanted to find a quiet country town for them to move to.

Meanwhile, a lady from a flower shop a few doors down from Solly's shoe repair shop had been fundraising for them and had raised more than $1,600 for Solly and Sarah.

When everything was finally in place, they loaded their meager possessions into Jeremiah's van and headed east until they reached the small town of Bensons Corner. Solly felt comfortable enough to stay there. Sun Valley Sawmill was located on the outskirts of Bensons Corner on a fairly large piece of land, where there was plenty of room for expansion. The sawmill employed between thirty and forty people and was owned by a man named Aaron Bentley McPherson, who was a fairly good employer, honest and careful with his dollars. He had a son named Edward with his wife who had died during childbirth. His house was a comfortable four-bedroom home on a bank overlooking a small creek that ran alongside the edge of the town.

Aaron came from a line of entrepreneurs, businesspeople who took a lot of pride in their successes as owners and managers and who most likely considered themselves as a cut above the average. The mill was fortunate to have a good supply of a fine variety of quality timber from a local forester. He had taken the time to scout around and had managed to acquire a large acreage close enough to the river to provide an area for good growth. He then proceeded to plant a variety of timber in the proper locations, and since this was all done at the turn of the century, the trees had plenty of time to grow. Therefore, by the time his grandchildren inherited the property, there were many nice stands of excellent timber.

grandchildren inherited the property, there were many nice stands of excellent timber.

THE TRAGEDY

Eddie McPherson was a normal teenager with a favorable attitude. He had a good friendship with a young lady who was a few months younger than he but was in the same class in school.

Sarah MacKeefer lived with her father, Solly, in a combination house and business just across a small creek close to Eddie's house. They had gotten into the habit of walking home together after school, and they really enjoyed each other's company.

One afternoon, Aaron, Eddie's dad, was at home. He was in a bad mood because Eddie had yet to clean up the leaves that had accumulated over the fall and winter. Aaron was a firm believer that everyone should do their share of the work, and when Eddie was too busy socializing rather than working, he couldn't resist making a comment. His choice of words was not only very hurtful but ended up being very tragic.

Sarah's family was certainly not the upper crust of local society, and Sarah was very conscious of this fact. That, and the fact that Sarah was a very sensitive and insecure child, made Aaron's comments all the more hurtful.

When Eddie and Sarah approached, Aaron said to Eddie, "Why can't you do your work instead of sitting around with some floozy?"

Sarah was on her feet in a flash, schoolbooks in hand, running across the creek over a small wooden bridge. Since it was early spring, the flow of the water was extremely high. As Sarah was running across the bridge, her right foot made contact with a small snag on the surface, causing her to swing sharply to the right and off the bridge headfirst into the cold, dirty water below.

Sarah was only under for a few seconds, but when she surfaced, she was already about fifty feet downstream, where the creek made a sharp right turn.

It was fortunate that a young fellow had been walking toward the bridge and had seen what happened. He saw Sarah coming toward him, and he entered the swiftly moving current in an effort to catch her. As she was passing by, he was able to grab her long hair.

In the meantime, Eddie had not only come running across the bridge but also made it to the creek, where the young fellow had hold of Sarah. Eddie was able to pull them both to the shore. Together they carried Sarah to a grassy spot nearby, but unfortunately neither of them was capable of first aid procedures, although it would probably have been of no benefit as Sarah had inhaled a lot of cold, dirty water into her lungs, and her prognosis was very poor.

Solly was informed of the tragedy, and when he arrived in the police car, he found Sarah on the ground with her head on Eddie's lap as Eddie kept stroking her hair and begging her to wake up; tears were flowing down his cheeks. "Sarah, please, please wake up".

The police could see that first aid was of no use so they proceeded to place her on a pad and covered her with a sheet as they waited for the coroner, who arrived shortly after. When the coroner had finished his examination, they carefully placed Sarah into a waiting ambulance to be taken to the funeral parlor.

Aaron McPherson arrived shortly afterward to take Eddie home, but his son angrily said, "Don't touch me! I hate you! You killed my best friend! Why? She never did anything to deserve that! You are a murderer!"

Aaron could see that nothing he could say would ever change his son's opinion. He also knew that in fact his own thoughtless and cruel comment had led to Sarah's death, although he had never intended to hurt her or anyone.

Eddie ended up going home with Solly to spend the night, and they tried to give each other comfort and support. Out of respect for Aaron, Solly had gone to his neighbors and phoned Aaron to let him know that Eddie was with him and that Solly would look after him. Aaron was at the funeral parlor the next morning, picking out the finest casket and making arrangements so Sarah's funeral would be done in the finest fashion.

The local residents, in response to the tragedy, were there in almost complete attendance. Jeremiah MacKeefer arrived toward the end of the next day, and with his arrival, the last pieces of the MacKeefer family fell into place.

THE FIRE

Bensons Corner was located in a small plateau consisting of two flat levels, one of them about thirty feet above the other; obviously when the ice was moving in the Ice Age, the thaw had arranged them in that fashion. Sometime during the Ice Age, the flows had created a cleft in the top shelf, resulting in a fairly wide channel, starting about twelve feet wide at the top and narrowing to about eight feet wide at the bottom.

The youth in the town had widened the channel to around twenty feet wide, and since it was composed of tightly packed sand and clay, it was quite stable and could be molded into whatever one desired. On that basis, the younger teen boys took out a substantial amount of soil from an area at the back in order to form themselves a nice room, where they placed some chairs and an older table.

In this way, they made a small meeting place for themselves. The opening in the front was only about four feet wide, and when some saskatoon bushes took hold on the sides, they provided the kids with some excellent screening.

Since it had been a fairly moist year, the bushes thrived, and a good mat of grass was growing on the path to their open door. Now that summer was over, the grass had dried right up, and all the leaves on the bushes were also dry.

That afternoon there were three boys in there enjoying their private smoking session. Charley Threinen, at fourteen years old, was the oldest; Eddie McPherson was thirteen, and so was Ryan Smythe. The obvious conclusion was that one of the boys flicked his still-burning cigarette out through the opening and onto the dry grass. Because of the natural flow of air through the opening and up the cleft, it would be reasonable to expect the cigarette to ignite the dry grass. The dry grass did indeed ignite, along with the leaves of the bushes. In moments, the opening of the meeting place was on fire, which was rapidly growing in size, trapping the three boys inside, fearing for their lives.

It was good fortune that at this time, Solly MacKeefer had gone for a walk in that direction and happened to be there at exactly the right moment. There was an old birdbath full of water on the side of the path, so Solly, realizing that there was no time to spare, went into action. He quickly stripped off his jacket and dipped it into the water of the birdbath. Then, throwing the jacket over his head, he charged through the flames and into the boys' meeting room.

Solly covered one boy with the wet jacket and charged outside, deposited the child, rewet his jacket in the birdbath, and was gone back inside once again. Moments later he dropped the second boy down, dampened the jacket, and was gone for the third boy. Dropping the last boy on the ground, he collapsed on his back near the birdbath. In the meanwhile, some women from a neighboring home had been involved in the process of using whatever clothes were at hand in wiping off the boys' faces and putting out small burning spots in the boys' clothing. Someone had shown up in a car, and they loaded the three boys into their car and took them to the hospital in the next town.

The women tried to make Solly as comfortable as possible by elevating his head and wiping his face with wet cloths. Solly, of course, was a terrible sight, with much hair and clothing burnt off, his eyebrows gone, and his face red and swollen, with his eyes almost closed shut. He reminded one of a squirrel who, in trying to escape a forest fire, had to go through some flames and had lost all his hair.

As he lay there on his back, he was breathing harshly as he had evidently sucked hot air and flames into his lungs.

It was at this time that Aaron McPherson showed up, as he had been informed that his son had been one of the boys in the fire. For a moment he did not recognize Solly, but when he did, he dropped to his knees, and placing his hands gently on Solly's shoulders, he tried to reassure him. "Hang on, Solly. The ambulance is on its way."

It almost seemed as if Solly had been holding on until this moment, as his eyes slowly opened halfway and his gaze locked onto Aaron's eyes. It was as if a message was passing between them for a few moments, and then with a slow, soft sigh, Solly's eyes slowly closed, and he was gone.

Strangely, in those last moments, a small smile formed on Solly's face, and it brought to mind stories of people who'd had near-death experiences of seeing lights, hearing music, and seeing familiar faces. Maybe in that instant, Solly could see his family, waiting to take him to where he belonged, on God's right hand.

Aaron seemed almost locked in that position for a few moments until finally he staggered up and made his way to his car. He sat there in deep thought for a while and then started his car. He slowly drove away to check on his son.

The coroner showed up shortly, followed by the ambulance, which loaded up Solly's body.

It was only three days until the funeral. It seemed like not only the local townspeople came to pay their respects, but there were many more people in attendance.

At the funeral, you would think they were burying some head of state or a famous entertainer by the size of the crowd and the news reporters. The most amazing thing was the obvious sense of loss that was evidenced by the local youth; people then began to realize the bond that had been established between the young people and Solly. He had always had a good rapport with youth, but when he lost Sarah, his relationship with youth grew and grew until it seemed he was closer to them than their own parents.

It had been like a regular Friday at the sawmill except that Aaron sent word around that he would like to have the workers knock off an hour early for a small meeting in the lunchroom.

When the workers had gathered, he proceeded to thank them for their years of good service and the performance of their jobs. When he started to speak, it became obvious that this was not the same Aaron Bentley McPherson that they had been involved with for so many years. This was what he referred to at the start.

"You are all very familiar with the young gypsy named Solomon Levi MacKeefer, who relocated to our town a while back and became a friend to our children. I'm sure no one gave much thought to that at the time, but I've had the privilege to get to know him and realize that he was properly named at his birth, or maybe he grew into that wisdom because of his name —whatever!

"The greatest quality I got to see in Solly was the greatness of his heart —and his kindness and compassion. I first met him through his daughter, Sarah, who was a schoolmate of my son Edward and one of his best friends. I got to know him later after I made a very cruel and uncalled-for comment that caused Sarah to leave our house in unnecessary pain and anguish, running for her home, which was the reason for her accident and the loss of her life.

"People have tried to reassure me that this was just a tragic accident, but I can assure you that I will have to spend the rest of my life with the knowledge that if it was not for my cruel, thoughtless comments, the accident would not have happened.

"One would expect that Solly would hold me to blame for the loss of his only child, and I would expect only that. I would not be surprised if he had tried to punish me for that. Instead, he punished me by smothering me with compassion and kindness.

"Yes, he did destroy Aaron McPherson, a man whose priorities were all wrong —wealth, prestige, a fine home, a fine auto, important friends, and so on. But he replaced it all with opened-up eyes and an understanding of the true values in life: kindness, compassion, friendship and family, and the beauty in the earth and the environment, especially if we can keep from destroying it because of our greed.

"The new Aaron McPherson is going to concentrate on those options, and as a result, I intend to get out of the sawmill business.

"As the community obviously needs the business to operate for the sake of our economy, I intend to sell the business. So my first option is to offer it for sale to the workers, who are the ones who helped build it up in the first place. The proposition is as follows: The mill is owned by a corporation, of which I own all the shares. If the workers desire to acquire the corporate shares and inform me of that desire, I will instruct my lawyers to make the changes necessary in order for each worker to buy a single share for one dollar, which will allow them to vote in order to allow the business to continue to operate and hopefully to grow. This would form a cooperative, which would give the business a better chance to survive and prosper." When he finished his proposal, he tm e to leave through the rear door and left amid a standing applause.

After his departure there was only a short discussion since the option offered was not only unexpected but exceedingly generous. The decision reached by the workers was 100 percent in favor, and a delegate was nominated to inform Aaron of that decision.

On Monday morning Aaron was at the attorney's office to carry on with the plan, which would create fifty new shares even though there were only thirty to forty employees, since this would allow some growth.

By Monday afternoon it became obvious that the workers would waste no time in cooperating with Aaron in the transfer, which was an obvious benefit to them. They had already picked Robert Matthews, who had managed the mill for the past two and a half years, to take the position of president. Susan Whitaker, the bookkeeper, would take the position of secretary, and they had already picked six people to act as an executive branch to help in major decisions.

The people were obviously in full support and couldn't wait to get the show on the road. Aaron was very pleased at the reception of his proposal.

It was a surprising move on a Monday morning when Ryan Smythe came up to his mother and asked her if she had some time to spare, as he had some thoughts he wanted to share with her. When she informed him that she had lots of time, he proceeded. Everything centered about the relationship he had with Solly even before the fire.

"Even before he saved our lives, we had a close relationship with Solly, and he tried to give us good advice about how we should pattern our lives. "I don't think he would want us to grow up as normal people; he would want us to be concerned about the important things in life. These would be integrity, a good relationship with our fellow man, kindness, and a respect for the environment. In the protection in the environment, there should be no hesitation in taking a stand. There is no benefit in making fortunes if in the process, we destroy our air, our water, and our land.

"His first concern was that we should respect our parents and also older people because our future depends greatly on their friendship and help. "First I wish to apologize to you and Dad for some of my behavior in the past and assure you there will be changes. Solly explained to us that Sarah's mother had been killed by young people who were addicted to drugs and could not control themselves anymore. This could happen to any of us. "Understanding this, our group has decided to stay away from all drugs as well as other bad habits. Smoking, for example, would cause major damage to our health, and we will quit such habits. We have heard rumors that Aaron McPherson got Lars Swenson to donate some prime land for the development of a ballpark and also room for parking and even room enough to build an arena. We would like to help these projects and therefore want to be in the best of health in order to enjoy them better.

"We have formed a group to this end, and we call this group the MacKeefers. It is a group of young people who want to work for the good of the community and make our parents proud of us."

On his way out, Ryan stopped to give his mother a big hug.

She couldn't keep her eyes from watering at this action. She could hardly wait for her husband to come home for lunch to share the news with him; she explained what Ryan had told her, and she shared her extreme relief and happiness with him.

Bob Smythe was a bit dubious, so he stopped by the fuzz shop on the way home and happened to run into Chief Tarrant at the office. When he came out with the question "Did you know we have a gang in town called the MacKeefers?" he was blown away by the response.

"Sure I do, and frankly, if you have a problem with them, you would probably be the one I would be throwing into jail. They are a fine bunch of guys, and if you drive around town with your eyes open, you will find the streets totally clean, with no garbage around. If you talk to their teachers in school, you will find there is a total change in their behavior, with teachers who are happy to come to school in the mornings.

"Another beautiful result was that bullying in the school greatly diminished, and it was again because of the teachings of Solly. When the boys saw bullying, they would question the bully why and then would explain to them that they should be aware that the victim could be, in fact, somebody's son or somebody's daughter. That psychology worked wonders, as the victims changed from being nobodies to becoming somebodies.

"There is one very striking point to look at in the case of a young girl named Sally, who was placed by Child Welfare in a temporary home with an older couple.

"She was only fifteen years old and had been sexually assaulted by a couple of youth, and though she could have gone to the courts, she obviously chose not to. When I asked some of the MacKeefers to keep an eye out for her safety, they went much further. They had a meeting and came out with a unanimous decision to adopt her, as the poor girl had no family.

"So in a very short while, she went from having no family to having twenty-three brothers. They presented her with a basic cell phone programmed so that she only had to press and hold one button, and seconds later she would have her phone ring on every one of her brothers' phones, and they would be in contact and ready to provide her with help.

"When she told me this," the chief said, "I couldn't stop my eyes from watering up. That kind and considerate act took a major concern from my mind."

The chief also mentioned to Bob that since the gang had taken a stand against all drugs, they would inform his office about anyone trying to traffic drugs anywhere in town.

After a fine supper and a lovely dessert, Ryan's family watched the news on TV for a while. As he was getting ready for bed, Ryan asked his father a very strange question: "Dad, do you know who owns the land where we had our little cave and our meeting place?"

When his father asked why he was concerned, he received a strange explanation.

"Solly was one of our very best friends, and that place is where we lost him. He had so much love in him and such a strong soul that we feel he may drop by and visit us at times. We thought it would be nice if we could build a meeting place there where he would be happy to come to."

His father did not hesitate to reassure Ryan that he saw merit in the idea and that it would be his first priority. Ryan thanked his father, probably surprised that his father did not think it was a stupid request.

The next day in a private conversation with his wife, Ryan's father explained to her that he could see no problem in the kids looking at life after death and that the idea of them having a meeting place of their own was an excellent idea, rather than hanging around on the streets.

Bob was as good as his word. In a couple of days, he had established that the area in question was the end of the street, and with the bank of dirt, there was no prospect that it could be used for anything in the future. He also gained massive support from other parents that providing a place for the youth to hang out in was an excellent idea and that everyone could work together to build a first-class place.

In no time they had acquired the donation of free work from a backhoe for excavation, and a plumber would donate labor and some materials. Masons, framers, and other tradespeople quickly fell in line, and there was no shortage of volunteer labor, so in no time, the project started to take shape.

The youth were blown away by all the support from the community and were always there to help out.

In the meantime, another example of their community spirit was in the case of Mrs. Robertson. Some boys saw her struggling with a couple of bags of groceries as she was walking home, and while helping her, they noticed that her sidewalk was in poor shape, and also there was no railing. So after discussions with their gang, this became their weekend project. They had no problem acquiring some four-by-four posts from the sawmill and some materials for the sidewalk. When they explained to the hardware store what they were doing, the owner provided screws, paint, and preservatives at no cost.

When they finished the job Sunday morning, there was a new sidewalk, and posts and railings were installed and painted up. When Mrs. Robertson was explaining to the chief, who had stopped to examine the results the next day, she had tears in her eyes. "These boys have restored my faith in the human race, and I enjoy my life again!"

The progress on the boys' headquarters was proceeding at a nice pace. In less than three months, they had their grand opening. It was obviously named Solly's Place, and it was equipped with bathroom facilities, a shower cabinet, and a sink, microwave, and fridge.

The people were blown away to see a framed poem in a prominent place; this was the message for all to see. The title was Abou Ben Adhem, and it went as follows:

"Abou Ben Adhem (may his tribe increase!)
Awoke one night from a deep dream of peace,
And saw, within the moonlight in his room,
Making it rich, and like a lily in bloom,
An angel writing in a book of gold :—
Exceeding peace had made Ben Adhem bold,
And to the presence in the room he said,
"What writest thou?" —The vision raised its head,
And with a look made of all sweet accord,
Answered, "The names of those who love the Lord."
"And is mine one?" said Abou. "Nay, not so,"
Replied the angel. Abou spoke more low,

But cheerly still; and said, "I pray thee, then,
Write me as one that loves his fellow men."

The angel wrote, and vanished. The next night
It came again with a great wakening light,
And showed the names whom love of God had blest,
And lo! Ben Adhem's name led all the rest."

There was also a picture of an emblem that the gang was working toward producing in the near future. It was a picture of a large heart, as that to them was the most important item. Across the heart were the words "Kindness, Compassion, and Courage," which were accentuated by a pair of balls hanging at the bottom. The message was that if you see someone commit some action that is unacceptable, you should have the courage to take a stand against it in whatever manner you can.

This was a poem that Solly had asked the boys to memorize. He said that if they could live according to those guidelines, they would have a good life and a lot of good friends.

In the meantime, Aaron McPherson was successful in his contacts with Lars Swenson, who owned acreage on the edge of town. Lars would donate to the community enough land to accommodate not only a baseball field and stands but also plenty of space for an arena and adequate parking.

Aaron had no difficulty asking people to donate to the community since he had already donated a working sawmill and thriving business. All these developments were very encouraging to the people in the community as prospects for the future.

In the midst of all the new developments, a very interesting event occurred.

The MacKeefer gang, who had provided their adopted "sister" Sally with a cell phone programmed to their phones as security for her safety, found that all of a sudden, all their phones started ringing.

Everyone responding was informed that while she was relaxing outside her home, two young lads were trying to convince her to go with them to a party and would not take no for an answer, and that she needed help.

Twelve-year-old Jimmy was the first on the scene, and he found that the two lads had Sally by the arms and were trying to force her into their car. Within minutes, a dozen more of the gang had assembled and had surrounded the car.

Jimmy was a couple of feet from the boys and demanded that they release Sally at once. When one of the boys made a threatening motion toward Jimmy, he was quickly informed by another of the gang members that if there were any harm to Jimmy, the lads would end up leaving in an ambulance.

When there was not an immediate response in releasing Sally, there came a smash as one of the headlights disappeared. This was followed by a bat smashing the driver's side windshield, the disappearance of the other headlight, and a rock smashing the rear window.

By then, the boys had gotten the message, and with a lot of swearing, they let go of Sally and proceeded to get into their car and leave. However, in the meantime, one of the gang was on the phone to Chief Tarrant, informing him that the boys had been trying to abduct Sally and that they should be thrown in jail and also that the car they were driving was not fit for the highway. The chief said, no problem, it was going to be under control.

Within a few blocks the damaged car was pulled over, and a wrecker was contacted to remove it from the road. The boys ended up in a cell and were allowed to call their parents to tell them they could end up being charged with attempted kidnapping and assault.

The chief had dropped by the scene and witnessed the bruises on Sally's wrists and had photographed them. When the chief returned to his office, he received the message that the lawyer for the boys' family had called demanding the release of the boys immediately or there would be a lot of trouble. The chief then contacted the lawyer to inform him that there already was a lot of trouble and his client's boys were right in the middle of it. He informed the lawyer that he had thirteen young people who were prepared to go to court to testify about the kidnapping and that he had pictures of the assault from the kidnapping attempt. He suggested that the lawyer would be wise to bring his client and come down to the station.

When the lawyer arrived, the chief's explanation to the lawyer was simple and basic: that these thirteen boys who had adopted Sally were adamant that the assailants should be charged and end up in jail for their crime or, at the very least, pay a substantial fine. He further explained that if the matter went through the courts, the young lads would have that on their records and would have major problems the rest of their lives. Knowing that the witnesses were trying to raise money toward the construction of a new arena, the chief suggested that maybe their parents could donate money to that cause instead.

After consulting for a short while, the boys could see the benefit in that; they came up with a figure of $20,000, and the chief agreed that they would then be willing to let it drop. If the parents wanted to take the easy way out and came up with a certified check to the Benson Corners Arena Fund, then that would be the end of the issue and the boys would have no criminal record.

The parents could see the benefit in that, but being frugal, they sent over a check for $10,000, hoping to save some bucks. The offer was totally rejected by the gang, and the response was that the chief would hang on to the first check and that the parents would provide another $20,000; that was a final decision, or else the courts would be the only other option.

The chief pointed out to the lawyer that with the courts, the parents could spend that much or more; the main fact to consider was that by donating the money, they could deduct it as a charitable donation and gain a tax benefit. The lawyer was back the next day with a certified check for $20,000, and the lads were released from jail. The most interesting part was that the lawyer left a check for $1,000 of his own as a donation. The news spread throughout the area, and that helped greatly in spurring on the flow of donations.

With all the great work done by the community toward a new arena, it was a pleasant surprise that a member of parliament was able to do his part and was happy to come up with a grant for $125,000 toward the project, which was excellent news for the MacKeefers and the community.

When a mother asked her son why the MacKeefers were so concerned with Sally's well-being, he explained, "We regard her as if she was somebody's daughter, and besides, she has nobody else to look after her." His simple and honest answer blew her away and brought tears to her eyes. She wanted to find some way to help keep the kids' minds and hearts pure and unpolluted into the future.

The gang's meeting place was done and in use when another situation arose: a young couple with a six-month-old daughter happened to arrive in town in a car basically out of gas; they had no food and were very much in need of help, including a place to sleep. Chief Tarrant proceeded to send them down to the MacKeefer layout. When they arrived there, it did not look too promising, but in no time, the boys started to show up. A mattress was brought for the family, along with a crib, complete with bedding and diapers. As things were getting organized, other boys emerged almost like magic, carrying trays of hot food and milk for the young one.

By the time the supper was finished, the place had warmed up into a comfortable home. Once the boys had their TV reception organized, they disappeared almost like magic after wishing the young couple a good night. When the couple woke up in the morning, they found that a pot of coffee and some breakfast were already there for them.

When it was time for the couple to leave after receiving hugs and good wishes from the gang, they found that their car was filled with gas. When, with tears in their eyes, they tried to thank their good Samaritans, the boys explained simply that it was okay as they were MacKeefers.

When the couple arrived at their parents' house late the following evening and after a night's rest, the wife made her way to the local newspaper and explained in detail their last few days to a reporter.

In her comments she made a statement to the reporter: "When we arrived at that town, we were broke, hungry, and totally in despair. By the time we left the next morning, we had a renewed faith in our world, and I told my husband that I had found my new family and I wanted to come back as soon as we could. He fully agreed. It was not only the gang of boys but the whole community that made us feel very welcome and at home."

She was pleasantly surprised to see in the next issue an article with the headline "What Is a MacKeefer?" A recounting followed of her and her family's experiences of the previous days. The reporter had made a special trip to the town and had not only talked to the police chief and some of the boys in the gang but spent the day wandering about the town. His comment upon his return was "If we could somehow send some of our world leaders to some classes at a MacKeefer school, then we could end up living in a much more beautiful world!"

After the very positive story in the city newspaper, which incidentally was picked up by the national news media, there were other major beneficial responses.

A retired architect who had been involved in the construction of other arenas and had various prints in his possession offered to come and help supervise the construction at no cost to the community. There were many other businesses that provided volunteer labor, discounted material costs, and so on, enabling the project to carry on at a very affordable rate.

With all this help, the arena was completed in record time, opening a week before Christmas much to the delight of the participants and customers. The member of parliament was there enabling himself to share in the glory and making a brilliant speech praising everyone for their ability to work together as a team and for their accomplishments.

It was around this time that there was a suggestion to change the name of the town from Bensons Corner to MacKeeferville, a suggestion that was almost unanimously approved. It seemed like ever since they'd lost Solly in the fire, there was a special magic in the air that helped to get the people in the community to bond together, and they all seemed to benefit from it.

With the new arena and ice, it was inevitable that hockey competition began to flourish, and it was only a matter of time before an ex-NHL player volunteered to coach a team. He was a star player who'd had to retire early because of a major injury, but he knew the game well and still loved to be involved. It became apparent early on that the local boys, because of their abstinence from tobacco, drugs, and other poisons, had grown up on the average taller, stronger, and faster and, because they had protected their minds, a little bit sharper.

The coach, having been injured because of violence in the game, trained his players to avoid violence and to concentrate on skills so that if they suffered being attacked, the best way to retaliate would be to go out on the ice and score a goal. This kind of philosophy enabled them to be more successful, but the main thing was that the game became more enjoyable. Altogether, there seemed to be more and more people wanting to move to MacKeeferville.

There should be a major concern that today's politicians have the bad habit that all their decisions are based on what would be of benefit to them in time for the next election. People should study the seven generations' teachings, which are based on anIroquois philosophy that the decisions made today should result in a sustainable world seven generations into the future. It is a philosophy that indigenous people have used for centuries, in relation to not just the earth but all decisions: How will this act affect the people seven generations from now?

The cup in MacKeeferville was not half-full but, in fact, filled to overflowing, especially after the community had drained out the negativity that the adult world had placed there. It was filled with the positivity of youth and their dreams and their visions for the future. They could see the beauty of the world around them and the potential to save the environment from the greed and shortsighted vision of society.

Having a few spare days on his hands, Aaron decided to make a final trip to the city to have a last visit with the owner of the large lumberyard, who had been his main customer. Through the years, he had always taken Sheldon and his wife out to a fine evening, but when he arrived there on his announced trip, he was informed that this time, they would spend the evening at Sheldon's home instead.

After complimenting Aaron on his action in the reconstruction of his business and the increased quality and performance of the sawmill, they had their meal. Aaron had lovely barbecued steaks and lobster tails.

Sheldon commented how much easier it was to do his business when there was customer satisfaction. After a relaxing dessert, they showed Aaron his bed in the spare bedroom and told him he could retire when he desired.

When Aaron finished a fine breakfast the next morning, he was informed that the boys had taken his car to the car wash. When he got in it to go, he was surprised to see that not only was it spotless inside but they had also filled up his gas tank.

On his drive home, he marveled at the kindness and consideration he was receiving from all sides. Only a few years before, he had been a lonely old businessman with very few really good friends, and now that he was much poorer, he felt like a king.

With that came the realization that all the change came after his association with Solly. Then the question came to mind as to whether Solly had born as wise as Solomon or whether there had simply been a fertile base where the wisdom took hold and grew.

The truth of the matter was that Solly had not only destroyed a lost old man but helped rebuild him into something wonderful to behold. He had also taken the youth of the area and, through patience and example, had turned them into something they could be proud of; they were a shining example for others to follow.

It is obvious to those who look around that if there is any hope for the world, it will be mainly through our younger generations' hope and vision, not through the shortsightedness and greed of too many of the older ones.

As Bud and I sat there at day's end with Bud sipping on a beer, I commented that with Bud informing me of all the area's highlights, he must have lived through it all. He proceeded to point to a picture over the counter, of a couple and two children.

He explained to me, "They all call me Bud, but it's only a nickname because that's the name of the draught. My name is actually Edward McPherson, and Aaron McPherson was my father. The woman is my wife, Melissa; the boy is named Solomon Aaron McPherson; and my girl is Sarah Melissa McPherson. And that is why the business is named Solly's Bar and Grill."

I was pushing my sixties and had been traveling the land looking for something, and now I had obviously found it and I was home. When it would come time for them to plant me, there were some lovely sights on the bench overlooking the valley where I could rest in peace.

ABOUT THE AUTHOR

The author having been born in Canada and having spent his more than 93 years involved in various activities here. From working on a circus, and the deckhand on a boat hauling grain on the great lakes, after years, being a ride operator on the carnival, to be assisting as a seaman on a rescue operation on the Pacific Ocean during a very violent storm in the fall of 1955. During his life, he was always involved in charitable activities and continues with that and he processed to donate $1.00 from each of his book sold in continuity to charitable operations.

9 798889 676393